Advance Praise for The Lioness Tale

Story and metaphor are an excellent and much deeper way (than psychology, or education or sociology) to speak to the dilemma and horrors of our time and to speak to the heart of people across ages and cultural gaps. The spirit of Lioness is strong and beautiful. I can well imagine how deeply her story can touch, reach and heal.

—Jack Kornfield
Author of "A Path With Heart" and "After the Ecstasy, The Laundry"

I found the narrative continually engaging. With something so highly imaged and a topic so explosive, it is to Diane's credit that the reader does not feel overwhelmed...
The analogy or the allegory is consistent and only one who knew her intentions would have begun the text with such understanding in mind. For someone who began reading without any preparation, it would have taken some time before it would have dawned on them that this is much more than a story of lions. That to me is a sign of the artistry involved.

—Jake Empereur, S.J
Author of "The Enneagram and Spiritual Direction: Nine Paths to Spiritual Guidance"

Wow! I loved it! Diane has written a beautiful and inspiring story and I'm sure the Universe will find a way for her to share it.

—Sita Lozoff
Co-founder of Human Kindness Foundation, sponsors of the Prison-Ashram Project

The prose alone would sustain the book because the prose is fine. I also like the metaphysics...I have worked a lot trying to get I AM concepts to convey their power to a reader. Good Luck!

—Helen Palmer
Author of "The Enneagram: Understanding Yourself and Others In Your Life"

What a magnificent description of the transformation/healing/conversion process. Diane's writing is full of deep spiritual power, wisdom and presence.

—Sandra Yarlott
UCC Minister, Director of UCLA Medical Center Chaplain Services

THE LIONESS TALE

For Brian

— a Diamond One
in the lines of
many —

with gratitude

THE LIONESS TALE

By
Diane Pendola

iUniverse, Inc.
New York Lincoln Shanghai

The Lioness Tale

Copyright © 2005 by Diane Pendola

iUniverse books may be ordered through booksellers or by contacting:

iUniverse
2021 Pine Lake Road, Suite 100
Lincoln, NE 68512
www.iuniverse.com
1-800-Authors (1-800-288-4677)

Graphic design concept by Diane Pendola

ISBN-13: 978-0-595-35139-8 (pbk)
ISBN-13: 978-0-595-79841-4 (ebk)
ISBN-10: 0-595-35139-5 (pbk)
ISBN-10: 0-595-79841-1 (ebk)

Printed in the United States of America

This story is written for imprisoned women everywhere.
Whether the bars that hold you exist within or without,
this story is dedicated to your liberation.

I want to particularly thank the women from the
California county jails and prisons
whom I have worked with over the years.
This is your story.
Thank you for entrusting it to my telling.

And most of all I want to thank
The Diamond One in my life,
Teresa Hahn,
without whom I would never have found my voice.

Foreword

ॐ

By Hal Zina Bennett, Ph.D.

Long ago, before the printed word was invented, storytelling was the primary way a community shared its wisdom. All members gathered around their leaders who told the tales that offered their knowledge and their magic. Sometimes the whole community also participated in dances or music-making that expressed their concerns, bringing up issues that reflected on the past even as it offered insights into current events. If the community depended on hunters, for example, the stories they told might deal with why there were no deer to be found along their usual hunting trails. This concern might also be expressed in a dance. Similarly, in an effort to find a solution to that problem, a storytelling elder might tell about great hunters from the past and what they'd done to bring the game back.

Today we have all but forgotten how important storytelling can be. We have forgotten how stories can unveil hidden answers to core questions about our lives. For those early communities, storytelling entertained, just as it does today. But the purpose of making and listening to stories was not the same as it is now, with television and movies, sophisticated special effects, highly developed acting techniques, and film-writing that is so visceral and sensational that we can literally forget who we are.

Today's TV and movie stories are usually intended as diversions, allowing us to escape our everyday lives. For storytellers of the past, it was just the opposite. In ancient times, storytelling took us deeper into our lives, not outside them. It helped us to connect with each other, the environment, and even the spiritual world, in a more intimate way. Storytelling was the very foundation upon which the health of a community was built. Stories pointed out that everyone's collective strength, safety, and general well being were dependent on each individual's ability to live up to their greatest capacity—to be the best their life could be. Stories informed, inspired, and explored ways that would make it possible for both individuals and the community to thrive at physical, emotional, and spiritual levels.

In *The Lioness Tale*, the author draws upon ancient traditions of storytelling. The story she tells addresses issues of living under conditions that are cruel and indifferent to the inner life of the individual. Most of us can easily identify with the Lioness of this tale. Though we are not, like her, animals torn from the wild and forced to live in cages, we know what it is to live in a world that is indifferent to our inner lives. We know what it is to long for the intimacy of a caring voice, of someone in our lives who knows who we are and believes that who we are is important.

Without stories like *The Lioness Tale*, we might go through our lives not even knowing what our longing and loneliness are about. There is much heartbreak in this story, even anger and a sense of outrage. At one and the same time we find ourselves wanting to reach out and strike out. We long to *reach out* to those who might ease our pain. We long to *strike out* at those who would dishonor us. Every cell in our body protests our constraints and repressions, whether they happen to be caused by our physical incarceration or by the imprisonment of our own thoughts.

Best of all, *The Lioness Tale* offers answers. But I must warn you, the wisdom you'll find here does not simplify the challenge it takes on. It acknowledges the deep pain of loss, alienation and fear. But so, too, does it bring us back to our own strength, our own safety, and ultimately our own voices. This is a storyteller who risks much by daring to tell the deepest truth of all our lives, the truth of finding our own hearts, our own souls, our own vulnerability and love. Her mission here is not simple entertainment. Rather she maps out a new path we can follow to greater intimacy, wherein we connect with ourselves, each other, and with forces greater than ourselves, forces that bind us all as one.

Readers of this story beware. This is not always easy reading. There are lessons that will change your life. Just as the author has dared much in the telling, you must dare much in the reading. You'll share the grief of the Lioness' loss both of love and her own freedom. But the reward you'll share is renewed inner strength and a sense of vulnerability by which you will get back your own life and celebrate it.

—Hal Zina Bennett, Ph.D, author, lecturer and consultant

In the beginning was the Word;
the Word was with God
and the Word was God.
The Word was the true light
which illuminates all who come into this world.
And the Word became flesh
and lived among us.

—John 1: 1, 9, 14—

Light in itself is darkness, cannot be seen, is invisible:
in order to become luminous, it needs me, an opaque body. Without me,
light would indeed be darkness,
And without light I would be nothing.

—Raimon Panikkar—

The
Lioness
Tale

Prologue

Once upon Timefullness, all is a limitless expanse of Space. Imagine the most wonderful velvet feel. Imagine a deep, rich, luxuriant blackness beyond imagining. There is no fear in this black spaciousness, no struggle in this expansive beingness. It just is. And within it lies the potential of all that might come to be. Every form is latent here, waiting for the Light from which it receives its unique Life.

From this black velvet Space the story of Lioness takes shape. It is here that the Light finds her, calls to her. She feels a stirring take place in the darkness, a desire to respond to this Light that is calling her name with such Love. Her response begins to take on a form. Large golden paws join long forelegs, which stretch into muscled shoulders; a strong neck supports a regal head from which two eyes gaze out like fiery suns each spinning around a black center of infinite peace. Her back is long and elegant and slopes into haunches that ripple with power. Her underbelly is soft and covered with fine white and yellow hairs with the feel of feathered down. She shakes her great head with the sheer exuberance of life and bounds through that Great Space, her rightful home, with power and grace. The Light is within her. She is the Light. Through this Light she has come to be. She is Lioness. And she roars the sacred sound of her name through that Space the way waves rolling in from the deep sea might roar upon the shore.

And now it comes to pass that upon the shores of time she is carried from that timefull place. She is born. And with the memory of the Dark and the

Light forever reflected in the orb of her fiery gaze, she enters the world of beginnings and endings.

CHAPTER 1

In the beginning was her Mother. Her mother licked with rough tongue all over her cub's body. Over and over her mother's tongue moved across Little Cub's eyes, washing away the grains left in the corners by sleep, washing down her nose and across her lips, licking away the sweet milk crusted at the corners of her mouth. Her mother's rough tongue smoothed Little Cub's soft fur, waxed it until it shone gold. She was the Mother. She offered Little Cub her warm belly, her warm milk, while constantly her keen eyes kept watch. Protecting. Protecting her cub from harm. Mother's paws were wide, her claws sharp, her teeth gleamed white. But her red tongue bathed Little Cub, lulled Little Cub into sleep, as she nestled in the warmth of her mother's breast close to her beating heart.

In the beginning she was safe. And in that safety she still floated in the awareness of the Space before time. In her dreams her tiny paws trembled as she remembered with what power she moved through that spaciousness of her rightful home. She remembered who she was: Lioness! Called into the world by the Light!

But as time passed, she grew bolder. The newness of the world drew her curiosity to explore every taste and smell and crack and crevice of her new home, and she began to forget her Self. All too quickly the knowledge of herself as a Sacred Being receded and she came to believe herself to be as her mother and the other forest animals treated her: a small, very curious, but quite dependent cub.

The world was such a rich and wonderful place. She stuck her little black nose into everything. Every creature's nest was investigated, every hole and crevice explored. She discovered that some creatures scurry and run like the mice. And they were great fun to chase and catch between her paws and hurl into the air! She found that some creatures stand and fight, like the badger. And it was best to back away, with her ears flat against her head, her little teeth bared, putting the best face possible upon her retreat. And some creatures just lifted up their tail and sprayed her with the most horrible odor, like the skunk. The smell made her sneeze and cough and roll around in the dirt for hours. But her Mother was never far away and whenever Little Cub came too close to danger her Mother's fierce roar and powerful presence was enough to make the whole world right again. Little Cub would safely strut and growl in the protective shadow of her Mountain Lion Mother.

CHAPTER 2

It was a beautiful autumn day in the forest. It was a day of endings. The wind had awakened from the sleep of summer to speak clearly in the rustle of the oak leaves, to whistle through the needles of the pines and alternately roar and sigh in the waving tops of fir and cedar. The wind whispered to the maple, "let go…let go…" and the maple shivered the whole length of her trunk, trembling each of her branches, sacrificing her garment of leaves in a brave shimmer of yellow and gold. The leaves drifted so gently, carried on the back of the breeze, catching the rays of the sun like the wings of a hundred fluttering finches, on their way down to soften and clothe the cold ground.

Little Cub loved to frolic in the deep leaves. She especially loved to lay on her back and throw the leaves up into the air swiping at them with her paws and catching them in her teeth as they came down. Then she would shake her head ferociously as though she had the triumph of some sweet prey in her mouth.

She had been born in spring. Now the crisp clean scent in the autumn air seemed to stir the heat in her blood. Although the awkwardness of adolescence was upon her, she could sense the power that was developing in the muscles beneath her skin. She could sense the strength that constituted her very bone and marrow. And the excitement of it stirred way down deep in her belly, gathered force and courage as it reached her heart and ached for the briefest moment in her throat until she opened her jaws full and wide and released into the world her Lioness voice. For the longest moment the roar filled the space between the earth and the cloud strewn sky, between the trunks of the trees. It joined the wind and became one with it. But in the silence that followed, another sound, foreign and fearful, split the air! Little Cub's mother, who had been crouching to drink at a nearby stream, collapsed. Blood poured from a wound near her breast, drenching her golden fur, soaking into the ground and running in red rivulets to cloud the clear water.

In an instant Little Cub was on her feet and running, running, running. She did not run toward her mother but away…her mother's dying image on her heels like a whip, like a fire, propelling her faster and faster away from the horrible moment, the horrible reality. She plunged ahead blindly; driven by a terror she had never before known. Never had this hot fear, this heart pounding panic ever coursed through her veins. And there was nothing else but this, driving her deeper and deeper into the forest.

Oblivious to the warning calls of birds, the alarm of the wind, she ran. She ran unwittingly towards the place where the earth was raw, where a trap had been so cleverly covered with the severed limbs of trees. She ran until the ground gave way beneath her and she plunged into the pit that the Strangers had dug for her capture. They had wanted, not the ferocious mother, but this youngster who would bring a good price on the black market. As Little Cub plummeted down into her living grave, terror ripped the spirit from her body. Then all went dark.

CHAPTER 2

✿

Little Cub slipped into the sleep of self-forgetting. The young Lioness had no memory of the pit, nor the terrible ordeal of her capture, nor the terror of being transported in a black box on wheels for many days journey. She had no memory of her life before the pit either. Her mother, the feel of the soft earth beneath her paws, the excitement of discovery, the voice of the wind were all forgotten, and with them, her Self.

Now her world was a ten by twenty-foot cage. She had come into the bloom of her maturity like this, living in a series of cages. They all had been more or less the same, all tended by Keepers, some of whom were kind and some of whom were cruel, but none with eyes to see the truth of whom she really was. And looking into this world of other caged animals and the Keepers that guarded them, there was none to reflect back to her that truth or to recognize the meaning of the Black and the Light in her fiery eyes. Instead she looked out and saw meanness and pettiness and cowardice. And thus she found herself to be mean and petty and cowardly.

She spent her days pacing, pacing, pacing. During the day there was no private place to be away from the staring eyes of the Strangers. They came every day and stared at her through the bars of her cage. From a distance they pointed or laughed. There were even times she saw a few cry. But all of them eventually turned their backs and walked off, leaving her alone to pace the night away. But even the nights were not her own. The Keepers were always skulking nearby. And there were Keepers who would sneak into her cage at night to tease and prod and beat her into an impotent rage.

She felt the rage in her belly. It was constantly there, like a red-hot wedge of iron, alternately burning and piercing. The Keepers said she was a strange kind of lion. Not one of them had ever heard her roar. She came to be called "The Silent One." Perhaps it was for this reason that the more sadistic of them would enter her cage at night assaulting and humiliating her, for they knew she would make no sound, and they reveled in their power. And with each humiliation her rage grew until she was sick with carrying it inside and longed for release.

In her dreams she would stand over them with a power that was foreign to her in waking. They would look with terror into her eyes and their abject fear would heat her blood to boiling. Then she would feel the rage begin to gather in her belly and plunge into her heart. She felt the power! But every time the roar would reach her throat it would explode inside her. Then it would be she looking up with eyes of fear and subjugation.

The bad dreams haunted her sleeping. The staring eyes of the Strangers haunted her waking. The Keepers constantly kept watch. And her prison grew stronger—not without but within.

CHAPTER 4

※

Time passed until there came a day of tremendous commotion among the Keepers. An edict had come down from some higher authority. It said all of the animals must be moved out of their cages and allowed to live in a way that was more akin to their "native surroundings." They said the conditions the animals were living in were "inhumane." The Silent One had never before heard these words "inhumane" and "native surroundings." But she came to understand that inhumane meant the animals were living in filth; that they were sickly and prone to disease because they were forced to live and eat in the midst of their own waste. She came to understand that inhumane meant that their food was not fresh, their meat was often rotten and their water polluted and unfit to drink. She learned that inhumane meant that the animals were not allowed to exercise, to develop the strength in their muscles and the natural intelligence of their minds. She turned this new word over in her mind: inhumane. And knew the truth of it in her bones. Who was this higher authority that named this truth? And what was the meaning of "native surroundings?"

The Keepers growled and whispered among themselves: "*Stupid damn politicians, don't they know if we keep these animals strong and healthy they'll turn on us?*" Some replied, "*there have been too many complaints from the Strangers, the Bleeding Hearts, who say they will not pay money to see the animals in these kinds of conditions!*"

There were many opinions about the new plan among the Keepers. Some vented their anger and frustration on the animals, whipping and prodding them into the vehicles that would transport them to new compounds many miles distant. They called the new place where the Silent One was heading a "Preserve". And although the Keepers cursed the political authorities beneath their breaths, they followed the orders to the letter and soon had all but the meanest and most ferocious of animals ready for transport. (These few "incorrigible" animals would remain behind in cages. It had been determined that these were beyond "rehabilitation" and the cages would forever be their punishment. But this is not their story).

The Silent One knew nothing of the authorities except that they had named the conditions she had been living in as inhumane and this felt true. Now she was being transported to a "Preserve," a place that was said to reflect her native surroundings, and a distant, vaguely remembered feeling began to stir in her heart. It was hope.

CHAPTER 5

During her first days in the unfamiliar compound the Silent One was very cautious. The new freedom frightened her. She had lived in such a small, enclosed space for so long that the expanse of open country that now surrounded her seemed full of hidden danger. She knew how to be alone. She knew how to survive in the solitude of her cage. But now she was thrown in among cats whose ways and languages were unknown to her. There were striped cats and spotted cats and cats in whose deep black coats the sun shone with a diamond light. She viewed them all as a menace and a threat and kept herself apart from them.

Over time the other cats grew in their respect for the Silent One. She was undoubtedly a big and powerful Lioness. But it was not her physical presence that intimidated. No, they sensed a tremendous inner power barely contained within her frame. It felt potentially explosive and thus they kept their distance, sensing danger in coming too close. And all the time the Silent One watched, keeping her fear contained in an outward stance of control and power. She understood that the one thing she could not show here was fear—or weakness—and her silent aloofness seemed to have the effect of keeping others away. It was a strategy that worked and as she identified with this new sense of power her fear receded and her influence within the compound grew.

She carried her territory with her no matter where she was in the Preserve. An invisible wall surrounded her, a field of energy that no one dared enter. There were a few challenges, of course, from other cats vying for power on the compound. But only one time did she have to fight.

A Tigress who had dominated the other cats, preying on the weaker ones and manipulating the stronger ones, approached her, growling and roaring. The Silent One became very still, very quiet as the Tigress escalated in her belligerent ranting. The Tigress, so caught up in her own sense of power, misinterpreted the Lioness' silence for weakness. She moved beyond the Silent One's invisible boundary, swiping with her great claw towards the Silent One's face.

All the pent up terror and rage of nights of humiliating assaults, days of numbing captivity and nightmares of powerless submission boiled into the blood of the Silent One. Her unvoiced roar energized every cell and every muscle of her being as she leapt at the Tigress, blindly unfeeling of the claws that sliced her own face and the knife edged teeth that penetrated her own neck. When she came back to herself she was straddling the Tigress. Her teeth, sunk deep into the Tigress' neck, were seeking the place where the blood runs thick and hot to the heart. She was so close to the kill she could taste the triumph. She was about to give one final shake of her great head, adjusting her jaw to clamp down on the place where the hot blood flows, when something even deeper than blood lust awakened within her.

She released her grip, withdrew her teeth from the Tigress' flesh and backed away, regarding the Tigress with eyes of deep sorrow. She gazed around at the other cats who had gathered in a circle. She had not known they were there until this moment. Their eyes were full of excitement and full of the taste for death that only moments before had thrilled her own being. She was disgusted—with herself—with all of them. The Keepers nearly had their triumph. Her fellow captives had nearly all been reduced to the base and cruel animals the Keepers believed them to be. She turned and walked away from all of them and entered into many days of great sadness.

CHAPTER 6

꧁꧂

The twenty-acre area of the Preserve that was allotted to the cats was totally enclosed by a high doublewide fence topped with rolls of thin metal with teeth sharper than a lion's in the prime of life. It was much too high to jump and the few cats who had been foolish enough to try had died terrible deaths, their soft bellies sliced through like butter upon the razor sharp wire. The terrain of the enclosure was rough and rocky. It was high desert country, freezing cold in winter and ablaze with shimmering heat in the summer. It was hardly "native territory" to the Silent One. But there were many outcroppings of rock and shallow caves where a cat could find relief from the torturous heat or a shield from the driving cold.

It was to such a shallow den that the Silent One retreated. The deep stirring in her Being that awakened her from her blind rage and lust for blood had also awakened something else. But this something else was unnamable. It was simultaneously something new and something ancient. It did not belong to her but rather possessed her. Her mind could not grasp it, although over the days and weeks she spent in her solitary cave, her thoughts chased it like an ever-receding ghost that always vanished just beyond her sight. The images in her dreams shifted. Liquid ambers and golds, forest greens and soft earth browns flowed into vaguely familiar shapes and forms of long buried memories. She would awaken with only fragments of a dream remembered: a pile of leaves, a sound of wind, a breath of cold. She would walk out upon the rock ledge of her cave, and as the sun arched its way across the sky, gaze out over the desert stillness, the black of her eyes searching backwards through time while the encircling light danced.

CHAPTER 7

The other cats gave the Silent One a wide berth. The sight of her, so still and quiet, silhouetted against the horizon from the sun's rising to its setting frightened them as much as her vicious encounter with the Tigress had excited and awed them. She was an odd cat—a loner—and so they left her alone. But there was one cat that watched her with neither fear in her heart nor awe in her eyes. She watched with the compassionate vision of one who has also suffered but who suffering has not vanquished. She watched with the wisdom of the Black Space spinning in the center of her deep golden eyes. She was a cat who remembered where she came from. She was a cat who had not forgotten.

She came from the land of the south where the sea met the rich luxuriant tangle of vine and growth of her native rain forest. This is where she had been born, with the constancy of the ocean an ever-present song upon her hearing. This is where her senses had grown keen, her ears sharp, and her nose sensitive to every changing scent upon the shifting winds. This is where she came to know the earth as her beloved, intimate with every furrow, cave and canyon that received the imprint of her great paws, every stream that quenched her thirst, every glen that nourished her and gave her shelter.

She was born into an ancient Pride of Panthers and raised wild and free. From the beginning she saw herself reflected in the eyes of the elders. She saw herself whole and complete in the mirror of their eyes.

She saw where she was in the surrounding gold. Every part of her was loved and affirmed.

Although she was as playful and curious as any cub, she would often withdraw from the antics of her siblings to gaze over the rolling sea. She could sit for hours. Long after her brother and sister had ceased their play, had nursed in the warm safety of their mother's belly and had fallen fast asleep nestled in the soft warmth of each other's fur, she would still be sitting motionless. For her the outer world had disappeared and she floated upon the inner world of Space like a white fleck of sea foam floats upon the sea, eventually to vanish.

The elders of the Pride watched her. As she grew, and as she continued to seek the solitude of the inner world, they knew that she was a cat with the gift of remembering, a Panther who would be a teacher for those who had forgotten themselves.

As the elders had watched her, now she watched the Silent One. Her spirit reached out to know her. She understood that the Silent One was in that in-between place where endings have not yet become new beginnings. It was a place like death. And like death it was a lonely journey. But she knew what the Silent One did not know. The Silent One was not alone. The Panther was holding her in the Love for which the Light had called Life into Time.

CHAPTER 8

Slicing down the very middle of the Big Cat's twenty-acre compound was a sheer cliff face. A cat walking among the sage and juniper would be startled to come upon the place where the earth gave way to sheer space. It abruptly dropped down hundreds of feet to an open valley of prairie and scrub oak. In this valley the male cats lived, separated from the females who inhabited the high table land.

From the slab of rock that extended out from the base of her cave the Silent One could look down into the valley of her brother cats. They were like a strange and foreign race to her. She had been caged during her adolescence and now, even here on the Preserve, the sexes were kept apart. But often their strong male scent and throaty growls carried upon the wind, raising the fur on her coat. She breathed their scent deep into her belly and experienced a yearning in the cavern of herself that longed toward the great cats below. The yearning gradually pulled her from her solitude. She began to pace up and down the entire length of the cliff's edge. Her ears forward in constant motion, her nose sniffing the wind, her eyes discerning the differences in size and shape and movement in the cats far below, her attention continually returning to one particular lion who began to match her pacing, stride for stride.

The Black Panther watched it all. She knew that the seed of remembering had been planted within the Silent One when she had retreated from the Tigress to enter into her days of watching and her nights of dreaming. The Black Cat also knew the seed had yet to yield to the life force so tightly held within its confining shell. There would be many moons rise to fullness and slivered away by darkness before the seed would bear its priceless fruit. The Black Panther watched as the Silent One began to enter upon yet another season of her life. But as the Panther knew, every season framed by the joy of beginnings and the sorrow of endings must pass.

CHAPTER 9

The Lioness and the Lion paced by day and hungered by night. The distance between them only intensified their desire. In their fantasies they scaled the treacherous wall each day to meet each other in a frenzy of passion and delight. In their hearts they transcended the chasm that divided them to rest in the love and the warmth of the other's cherished presence. In their bodies they felt the instinctual stirrings that lit their blood with fire and drove them to discover a way by which their love-heat might be quenched. Each of them, from their own perspective, searched every crevice of the cliff's face, seeking out those fissures where a cat might be able to inch a way toward union with the beloved. And after many days exploring, a way was found.

On the eastern rim, the cliff face was not so sheer. It was indeed steep, littered with rock and debris that rolled treacherously beneath a cat's feet. But there was a rupture within the bedrock that extended from the top of the cliff to about midway down. There the rock jutted forward, creating a jagged ledge about fifteen feet long and ten feet wide at its broadest point. A lone Juniper tree clung there, defying the hostile elements and battering winds. From this ledge another fracture in the cliff wall created a broken path down to the valley floor. It was to this ledge that each found their perilous way one moonless night. It was on this ledge that the Juniper bore witness to their wild and ruthless love.

CHAPTER 10

They met infrequently at first, but grew bolder as time passed. Even on nights washed in the light of a full moon The Silent One made the steep descent, risking the watchful eyes of the Keepers. The original fire that raced in her blood now became like coals smoldering in her very bone, a slow and constant lava flow in her marrow that erupted on the precarious ledge of their love-making with all the volcanic force of years of pent-up passions.

She became like one possessed. The other cats watched her. They watched her frantic pacing along the cliff's edge. They watched her grow gaunt. They saw the haunted stare that looked through them as though they were not there. They knew what was happening. She and her Lion were not the first pair to discover a lover's lair. There were other trysting places besides the ledge. And the Keepers were not blind. They had their reasons for turning away their eyes, for pretending not to see. But the Silent One was blind to the whispers the Keepers exchanged with each other behind cupped hands and deaf to the cautions of her sister cats.

She was obsessed with her Lion. She lived for the nights when she could feel his teeth tenderly and passionately upon her neck. She longed to surrender beneath his weight, to feel the deep rumble of his purr resound within her own breast. But his thrusting haunches did not quench the fire flow ignited deep within her being. The gripping desire of her inward core clenched and unclenched with unsatisfied craving long beyond the time his sex was spent. With each encounter her hunger only grew as though he had opened a great cavern within her that could never be filled.

Yet she longed for fulfillment. As her demands grew, he withdrew. At first it was a sullen aloofness she felt. He was cold. And his cold made her burn all the hotter. She would melt the icy wall that was growing between them! But the more she flung her fire toward him, the colder he became. Then there came a night when he did not come to meet her upon the protruding lip of rock beneath the Juniper tree.

CHAPTER 11

She continued to descend the cliff for nights afterwards. But never again did he come to meet her. She lay heavily upon the naked rock, the Juniper needles providing scant protection from the cruel cold. Looking out into those winter nights the stars shone, frozen and distant, against a great expanse of darkness. Who can say what kept her from plunging her body into that darkness, away from the icy claw extending its fingers all the way through her heart, to grip her very soul? Only her breath, hot upon the frozen air, lingered about her as evidence of warmth. Only her breath, an ephemeral mist upon the night wind, whispered to her of Life. She felt alone and betrayed, emptied of hope, a great hollow shell devoid of feeling. But there were moments when the shell cracked and she was released upon the breath to dissolve into the infinity of space.

Those moments passed. She forgot them. She pushed them down and back into the same dark regions where so much of her was buried. She preferred to remember the betrayal, to cultivate her hatred, to thicken the armor that she presented to the world as her self. The heat ceased to flow in her veins. Her blood ran cold.

The other cats in her compound spoke behind her back. They said her Lion found someone new, a Lioness less intense, less eerily silent. But none dared confront her. The Silent One felt more isolated, more alone than ever before. None would have guessed that behind the snarls she hurled at the other cats was a Lioness desperate for connection. Not even she would have admitted that the longing for fulfillment, that the

lion had awakened within her, lay wedged in the wall of her defenses like
a gate pried loose opened

CHAPTER 12

But the Black Panther knew. She watched with knowing eyes and with the patience of wisdom. She knew how to wait. The elders of her Pride had taught her well. They had seen to it that her natural gifts had ample opportunity to develop. They had encouraged her solitude and her inner journeying. There were times an elder would sit beside her in silence and journey with her into inner space where they would commune together in the oneness of their Being before Time. And there were times when all the members of the Pride would gather in a Sacred Circle under the Light of the full moon to contemplate together the Dark from which they came, the Light for which they were created and the Love which was the bridge between. These were sacred times of remembering for the Pride of Panthers. And through it all the young Panther grew in grace and wisdom. Panthers both young and old sought her out for the kindness she showed them and for the deep peace they felt in her presence.

Perhaps it was this that drew the Silent One toward her. The Black Panther had never spoken to the Lioness but the Silent One knew that the Black Cat was watching her. Surprisingly it didn't anger her. She felt comforted by those golden eyes. They held no judgment, no hidden intent. They were clear and somehow innocent. Over the days she circled closer and closer to the magnificent Black Cat. Her circling was so subtle, so cautious, that only one with the Panther's powers of observa-

Ann would have even noticed the steady and studied approach of the Lioness.

CHAPTER 13

And so it came to pass that the Silent One found a friend. In the beginning she put her friend through many tests, but never did the Panther betray her trust. Sometimes the Silent One raged. She snarled without reason. The hair stood up upon her back more often than it relaxed. But her anger found no fuel to ignite within her new friend's being. Rather, her snarls fell upon the Panther like a burning branch upon the water. In the Panther's presence she found relief.

She still walked the compound, a powerful loner from which the other cats kept a respectful distance. The bars of her inner prison kept others far away. Even the new cats sensed her invisible wall. But the same defenses that conveyed her strength and power to others concealed her tenderness, her vulnerability, and her needs to give and to receive love. She had shown her need to the Lion and he had betrayed her. Since he had abandoned her she had fortified her walls and retreated even further behind them. But somehow the Panther had slipped through the gate that the Lion had left fixed within her fortress. The Panther had come inside her and the Lioness let her stay.

※

CHAPTER 14

Nearly every part of the compound could be seen from the scars that crisscrossed the land. The Keepers patrolled the compound enclosed in metal boxes that rolled back and forth across the scars in a constant cloud of dust. They carried long pieces of iron that were capable of producing an explosive sound that made the Silent One's heart pound with terror. The first time she heard the sound, it was a warning shot, fired off to break up a fight between two cats on the yard. The Silent One, in sheer panic had fled at the ear-splitting sound, bolting blindly into the fence that surrounded the Preserve, hitting it with such force that she was knocked unconscious.

The Keepers, armed with their pieces of iron and accompanied by their dogs, had swarmed into the yard. Leashed and vicious, their dogs growled and snapped their way among the Big Cats. The Keepers, close upon their canines' heels, swung their clubs and threatened with their pieces of iron until the yard became quiet and the cats backed away, shamed by the domesticated dogs that sent them to their dens.

Several Keepers and dogs gathered around the unconscious Lioness. As she struggled to regain awareness she felt she was caught in a great net. She thrashed with her body and slashed out helplessly with her great claws, desperate for release from the net she imagined tightening with each futile movement. She felt as though she was being heaved up from a great black hole in a web that kept her penned and powerless. As she opened her eyes it was not the Keepers she saw but other Strangers and other dogs from another time. She gathered all of her strength to rend the ropes she sensed binding her body, to leap at the Strangers, to tear the sneering smiles from their faces.

What the Keepers saw was a cat gone mad. She felt a hot slice of pain in her right hip. Her body went limp and passed beyond her control. Her eyes stared helplessly at the Keepers as they dragged her to a cage where they slammed the door upon her and left her alone in stunned paralysis. She came to fear this power they had over her even more than she feared their long iron weapons of terror.

CHAPTER 15

They had kept her in the cage for several weeks. It was the worst kind of humiliation and slavery. The drugs they injected in her flesh twice each day stole away her pride, her mind and her very soul. More than once a Keeper came into the cage and violated every part of her body. He forced open her great mouth and she was powerless to close her jaws upon him. He thrust his fist into her anus, his hand into her vaginal cavity, probing and prodding and she was helpless to defend herself. She was like a dying carcass, like wounded prey, defenseless against the carrion birds that pecked at every orifice of her body.

When they released her from the cage, back into the so-called freedom of the Preserve, they said it was a privilege. They said they would cage her again if she even snarled at a Keeper. They said if she even looked at a Keeper wrong they would cage her for good and drug her forever.

This too had thickened the walls of her inner prison. Her rage smoldered inside her. The hope she had brought with her from the world she had known before the Preserve was consumed by hatred and a nauseous sense of betrayal. This place was not humane. It only appeared so to the Strangers who came in their boxes on wheels, who would stop and poke their heads out of windows and flash strange lights at the Big Cats and then roll back down the great gate of the Preserve, and away. They didn't see the cats that were kept drugged in cages more foul than the ones she had come from. They didn't know that the abuse here was subtler, more sophisticated, more hidden. They didn't know that the battle here was not for dominance over the Big Cats' bodies, but for ownership of their soul. Or did they? Did they even care? The Silent One came to hate the Strangers even more than the Keepers. At least the Keepers were part of the battle. They too had anger and hatred and sometimes kindness. But the Strangers only watched from a safe distance, from behind their windows. Sometimes the Silent One would meet their gaze with her own fierce stare. She would see fear spring behind their eyes, but it was quickly shuttered by indifference, by their capacity to drive away, by their capacity to forget.

CHAPTER 16

She found comfort in the presence of her new friend. She did not know why. Wasn't the Panther also a prisoner? Why then did she seem so free? The Silent One had no answers, just a growing curiosity about her friend whose beautiful golden eyes held such deep black centers.

Looking into the black of those eyes the Silent One was drawn more deeply into her own self. She was drawn into herself and beyond herself. She lost herself in those eyes. The anger, which formed the thickest crust of her defensive shell, collapsed beneath that gaze, the red of its energy drained as she dropped down into the layer below the anger, and down again into the layer below the fear, and down again into the layer below the sadness. She would drop deeper and deeper until there were no more layers, until she touched something that was true and real and alive. Then she would find her self again, but as something, someone totally new, totally changed, totally other than what she had believed herself to be.

This belief about who she thought she was would bring her back, as though from a dream. And she would shake the dream from her head and pull her eyes from the Panther's gaze and remember that she was a caged animal, a captive. Her anger would return. She would feel it taut in her muscles, set like a trap to spring on anything that might come too close. And she would withdraw then from the Panther. She would avoid her for days, nursing her anger as though the Panther threatened it, as though the refreshing waters of the Panther's presence might consume the raging fires of the Silent One completely. And then who would the Silent One be? Without her anger how would she survive?

This did not disturb the Panther. She knew that the seed so tightly enclosed within the layered shell of the Lioness was stirring with the power of new life. She also knew that when the Silent One looked into the Panther's eyes the Lioness beheld her own reflection there. It was her own deep Self that drew her. It was her own Sacred Being she touched. But the Silent One could not tolerate the greatness she discovered within. She believed herself small. She believed the lie she had seen reflected for so long in the eyes of all the self-forgetting Cats and Keepers and Strangers. She believed that lie to be the Truth. The Panther knew this. She offered the Lioness her eyes, her Self, as a mirror; a mirror that for the first time in the life of the Silent One could reflect back <u>all</u> of who she was.

But for the Silent One to remember who she truly was meant death to the Cat she believed herself to be. That Cat had begun to die the day her driving desire to kill the Tigress had given way to something deeper. What had it been? It had felt like some deep well of grief had opened up within her, deeper than her anger, deeper than the bloodlust driving her. It was a profound sense of loss for herself, for the Tigress, for who they once were and might be again. It had been the most poignant sorrow that drove her to her den. A vast emptiness had opened in her belly. She wandered that emptiness, feeling utterly lost. The Panther had recognized the moment of awakening. It was the quickening of the seed. It was the beginning of the Silent One's journey Home.

CHAPTER 17

The Keepers knew that the Silent One was pregnant. They had hoped for it! After all she was a magnificent specimen! And her mate was a strong, healthy, dominant male. He had fought the other young males of the compound for the privilege of scaling the cliff to meet her on the Juniper ledge. The Keepers had allowed the clandestine meetings. The two cats would produce beautiful offspring and there were Strangers that would pay a handsome price for the cubs!

The Silent One had been naïve and foolish to believe that the Keepers were unaware. The other cats had tried to warn her, but their warnings had fallen on deaf ears. She herself had seen the Keepers watching and whispering. But she had turned away from the whispers; had ignored the scent of danger—the very air thick with premonition—that the deepest sadness was yet to come.

The Keepers had verified the pregnancy during the time she had been drugged and caged. The one who had violated her had confirmed it. She hadn't known the purpose for his horrible presence. He had been cruel in his work as though her powerlessness unleashed a sadistic impulse to hurt and expose her far beyond the requirements of his duty. Beneath his ruthless scrutiny she was no Lioness at all, only an object to be penetrated by his caustic hands and probed by his cold instruments. She became an object of contempt, most tragically, to herself.

Now that self-contempt stirred as she felt the stirring of life in her womb. She had been a blind fool! She felt the Lion had used her. But now she saw that he, too, had been used. Their youth and desire and years of captivity had conspired with the malicious intent of the Keepers to render them breeders and incubators of life that could never be theirs. Now she saw too clearly the whole terrible truth: the Keepers would take away her cubs and she would be powerless to stop them!

CHAPTER 18

Do you know what it's like? Do you know what it's like to have the energy of youth in your veins, the vitality of strength and health course through your veins? Do you know what it means to have your very own life force beat you down as surely as your feet beat upon the concrete floor, a scar etched by hour after hour of impatient pacing? Do you know what it means to have this energy caged? Do you know how it flows like hot lava from the belly, hardening in the heart and exploding in red rage in the mind? And if you are female, and if you have carried within your womb the sacred treasure of a beating heart, of new life wrapped warm within the safe solidity of your own body, you know with what fierce mother love you would fight to bring that new life safely into the Light. And what if you were not allowed to fight? What if you were beaten down and back? What if you knew that the sweet, innocent life would only suckle a week? A month? What if you knew it would eventually be torn from your breast, crying and confused? What if you were helpless to follow...powerless to pursue, as you own life's blood was carried away from you, the screams growing fainter and fainter in the distance? Can you imagine how the screams might echo in your mind? How they might haunt your dreams?

The Silent One knew. The cubs were with her barely six weeks. She tried not to remember that moment when they were pulled from her. She tried to forget their anguished cries, the look of terror on their faces. She tried to believe that they knew she did not willingly abandon them.

She tried to console herself with the thought that somehow they would grow up with the memory of her stored in the cells of their beings. But she was haunted with the fear that they would only remember her failure; they would only remember her powerlessness; they would only remember the mockery of her as a mother.

CHAPTER 19

During the time of her pregnancy and afterwards, while her cubs nursed, the Silent One had been isolated from the rest of the Cats in the Yard. Then, she had been caged for her protection and that of her offspring. Now she was caged because she had more than snarled at the Keepers when they had taken her cubs away. She had thrown herself upon them, claws fully extended, fangs bared, a cat gone out of control and ready to kill. They had shot her then, with the tranquilizer gun. With the cubs held firmly within their grasp, the Keepers slammed the great iron gate behind them, turning the lock and pocketing the key. She collapsed on the cold floor of her prison, unable to command her muscles to move. The drug heightened the acuteness of her hearing as she listened to the fading sobs of her babies. Despair took hold of her then. All the colors washed out of her. The red of her rage drained from her mind's eye. The rose glow of love for her cubs drained from her heart. All went gray.

They drugged her for a few weeks after that. But gradually they came to see that the drugs were no longer necessary. The great cat no longer bristled at the Keeper's approach. Her gaze was dull and apathetic as though a lid had closed within her eyes. The proud and defiant cast of her great head was gone and now it hung low and lusterless. No longer was there rage when the Keepers entered her cage. And they seemed to do it more frequently now. The same Keeper who had confirmed her pregnancy seemed to be a weekly presence. He listened to her heart and shined a narrow pinpoint of light into her eyes. He opened her mouth and pressed his hateful fingers to her gums. He stuck needles in her veins, withdrawing her red-hot blood. And she gave without resistance, wishing he would empty her veins to the last drop so that she could finally die and be done with this living death. There was no fight left in her, no feeling. He could do what he wanted. She was broken.

CHAPTER 20

The Panther came each night. The black of her long, sleek body reflecting the star-strewn sky, she would glide through the compound like a ghost and stretch out at the foot of the Silent One's cage like an invisible spirit. The Silent One gave no sign that she was aware of her friend's presence. Yet the Panther never wearied of her watchful vigil.

Some nights passed in silence. The sound of the Panther's breath and deep throated purr blended with the song of crickets and the sage scented wind that blew steadily over the Preserve from the south. Occasionally it was punctuated with the hoot of an owl or the sudden cacophony of a pack of coyotes whose eerie howls, hurled against the desert expanse, would end as abruptly as they began. Before dawn drew a crimson line of meeting between land and sky the Panther would melt back into the dark as naturally as the twilight mist would soon be melting upon the first rays of day.

Other nights the Panther told stories. She told of her own youth, of her own days of living free. Her voice murmured across the short distance that separated her from the Lioness like a stream murmuring across stones. And without conscious knowing the Silent One was caught in the gentle motion of the stream, carried upon the Panther's words like a leaf floating down current toward the sea.

CHAPTER 21

❁

The Lioness curled in the corner of her cage. Months had passed since the loss of her cubs. Her hipbones protruded pathetically through her matted coat. And her cell was foul. She stared apathetically into the night, looking through the Panther as though she was not there. Yet the Panther was not disheartened.

"Imagine," the Panther began, "a land without cages, without Keepers and Kept, without meanness and cruelty. Imagine a land where the waters run gentle and clear over green hills and roar through canyons of towering rock walls carved by the winds and waters of time. Imagine the freedom to run the paths of the Ancients through tall trees, sunlight filtering through their canopy of branches, shimmering upon the mosses and ferns of the forest floor. Yes, you can imagine it, Silent One…Don't say, don't say you cannot even imagine…it is in you…the texture of the earth beneath your feet, the wind in your flaring nostrils, the scent of the forest and all its creatures filling your being. The earth is in you! And the rich land of your birth! Freedom is within you, Silent one."

The Panther paused, her attention caught by the slight forward movement of the Silent One's ears, signaling that the Lioness was listening. She knew the desire to live was flickering in her friend, if only dimly. She fanned the struggling ember with winds that blew up from her own life. "Imagine it all with me now, Silent one," she continued, "as I recall this ending of my youth.

- 44 -

I was protected in the Pride, cherished, nurtured, nourished by the constant presence of all around me. I had never been truly alone, never without the watchful eye of an elder holding my solitary play within their
protective gaze. I was never without meal, without water, without compan-
ionship. But now I was at an age, where I had the strength to take life and
the power to birth it. And according to the transition rites of my Pride it
was time for my journey into the wilderness, alone.

After wandering for three days without food I came to a great tree whose
center had been charred by a fire long before. There was a triangular opening in the tree through which I entered into its dry and sheltered heart. I
was hungry and tired, afraid and terribly alone. I imagined invisible ghosts
and hidden dangers ascending into the dark regions above me. But I drew
the ritual circle as prescribed in the rite that the elders had taught me and
intoned the ancient chant. The chant slowly, surely drew my awareness
away from my frightened scanning as I descended into my own center. My
breath, slow and deep and rhythmic, opened doors upon the inner world of
vision until I entered the dream.

In my dream I stood beneath a magnificent tree. It was strong, mature,
in the prime of life. Its roots reached deep into the earth. Its branches were
supple and dressed in the green leaves of summer. I parted the branches and
walked into their shade where I found myself confronted with a great
snake. His circumference was thick as a sapling and he was black like the
black of a star lit night. He was draped pyramid shaped among the
branches, his head poised in the center of the pyramid, eyes gazing directly
into mine, his red whip of tongue lashing the air about him. Our eyes met
and held as I absorbed my shock. I knew he was not malevolent, he meant
me no harm, yet he commanded respect through the sheer power of his
presence. I knew he was a great being and it was this greatness that made
me feel afraid. His voice came to me like a low whistle, like a hiss of wind
through a cleft of rock. It entered me as silently as wind, as surely as breath
it came inside and spoke to my trembling heart. It said:

'You are afraid. Rightly so, but not for the reasons you imagine. You fear
I could destroy you. But this is not my intention. You will feel as though you
are indeed dying through your contact with me. But it is the death that

gives birth to the conscious soul. And it is consciousness you fear. Yes, you remember where you came from. This is true. But your purpose here belongs to the realm of my teaching. Your soul has taken flesh. And in the world of flesh lies the necessity of choice. How will you choose?'

His voice blew through my heart, cool, expansive. A sense of freedom accompanied it—an awesome freedom. And worlds I knew nothing of opened before my inner vision. There were beautiful worlds and monstrous worlds, worlds of kindness and worlds of cruelty. As I wandered through each one of them I came to realize they were all within _me_. They were, all of them, in my heart. And with this awareness I was afraid. I wanted to run away. I wanted to hide. I didn't want to know the extent of my capacity for great evil _and_ great good. I didn't want to know what I now knew. I had lost innocence. The world would never again be the same. He said:

'You can deny me. And the very thing you seek to deny will possess you with the power of a demon. Or you can allow me to teach you. And my teaching will release the energy of life within you. I am the fruit of the tree of knowledge. And I offer you consciousness. Will you choose to remain a slave, asleep to the great purpose of your life? Or will you choose the path that will set you free? The choice is yours.'

My inner vision shifted again and I saw myself old. I saw myself in pain, my eyes failing, and my haunches no longer able to lift me towards my prey. I saw my death. And from the eyes of impending death I looked back through time. I saw my life, brief as the flash of a falling star through the heavens. How empty to spend it chasing after my own security as though I could keep death at bay. How futile to sell the precious pearl of my soul's wisdom for the transitory pleasures of a world in constant flux and change! I saw clearly, that at the deepest level of my being, true freedom consisted in not having any choice. Ultimately there was only one choice: the choice for Light, for Love, for Life. All other choices ended here in death and I with them. Only these could take me through death to the other side. Only these could take me Home.

From that moment, Silent One, I accepted Snake as my teacher. He whispers in my left ear, 'Do not be afraid of the Truth. The Truth will set you free.' And in teaching me Truth he teaches me to let _all_ of life in. He *instructs me that all life is my teacher. He reminds me of my capacity for evil and through it teaches me humility. He opens before me the territory of freedom and within that Promised Land, the power to choose my own path."*

The Panther ceased her speaking. She looked at the Silent One. The Lioness was no longer looking through the Black Cat but directly at her. Returning that direct gaze the Panther said:

"You live in a world of cages, Silent One, in one of the monstrous worlds. But you can wake up. You can wake up and choose your own path, even here. This is not greater than your own heart. Nor does it run deeper than your own soul."

CHAPTER 22

The Lioness heard the Panther's words. They penetrated into some sub-terranean part of her where they came to rest like gold at the bottom of a deep well. But more than her words, it was the Panther herself who affected her, whose faithful presence at the foot of her cage night by night radiated warmth that subtly, imperceptibly thawed the numbing cold which gripped her flesh. The Silent One's indifference slowly began to give way to anticipation. As weeks continued to crawl by, the nightly visits from the Black Cat became as essential to her as the meager rations of food and water she received each morning. The presence of the Pan-ther was food for her soul, the nourishment that was restoring her to life.

As she soaked in that sustenance she did indeed find a choice growing before her: a choice for life or death. But life was so painful! As her heart began to thaw it felt as though a knife was being plunged and turned into its soft center. The loss of her cubs was overwhelming. The tears that had frozen behind the lids of her eyes began to flow uncontrollably as she awakened from her wintry sleep. The grief heaved within her. It loosed, from the glacial fortresses of her soul, icy floes that cut her and left her feeling battered and defeated. The rivers of tears, raging from her loss, met other rivers within her, other rivers of tears flowing from even older wounds. It seemed as though the tears would never stop. She felt she was drowning in tears.

"*It's too much!*" She cried out to the walls of her cage.

"It's *too much*," she whispered to the Panther in the silence of the night, for the first time admitting her vulnerability to another living creature. She reached her paw tentatively through the bars of her cell, gently touching her friend's face. She looked into the Black Cat's beautiful golden eyes, searching there for a reason to go on, for a reason to live. The Panther met the gaze of the Lioness, held it, and invited the Lioness to come all the way in.

CHAPTER 23

The Silent One entered. She was drawn away from the concrete floor of her cage, away from the bars, away from the rolls of razor wire enclosing the Preserve, away from the barren land with its bite of dust in her mouth like a hot dry wind. She was drawn deeper and deeper, drawn by a force beyond her, the way a mountain stream is drawn by the distant sea. And she let go. Like a stone dropping through the currents of a river she dropped below the raging of her thoughts, she dropped below the swirling emotions of her heart, deeper and deeper until she reached waters still and calm. Through the door of the Panther's gaze she entered into waters hitherto unknown. And yet they were not deeper than her Self. No matter how deep she went she was still within herself, the way a wave is still within itself when it breaks upon the open sea...no longer merely a wave but also the sea, no longer merely a part but also the whole. She dropped deeper and deeper until she was the whole of the sea, and deeper still until she was the spaciousness that held the sea...and the stars...and the moon. She was exquisite spaciousness. And the space was infinite and soft and black the way velvet is soft and black. It was a soft black comforting velvet spaciousness without boundaries. And this too was her Self.

She rested a long time in this spaciousness. In this timeless realm she rested where she and the Panther were neither one nor two, but separate manifestations of a life force that joined them as members of one continuous Self.

When the Silent One woke that morning, dawn was lapping against the horizon with red and purple waves of light. Feathered clouds graced the morning sky with shimmering veils of gold. She watched the horizon until the sun crowned, radiant.

CHAPTER 24

Still confined to her solitary cell, weeks turned into months. But she did not feel alone. The Panther was a constant presence. When her body was not lying stretched on the earth beside the Silent One's cell, the Black Cat's spirit stretched to inhabit the space between them like a soft breeze. The Silent One looked forward especially to the deep nights, when the Keeper's eyes were closed in sleep, and her friend could continue to unfold the story of her life to the Lioness, mysteriously giving meaning to the Silent One's own life.

"There was something in me that knew the change was coming." The Black Panther's words reached into the past, as she smelled the faraway scent of Strangers landing upon the shores of her native home. She saw again the devastation that was to come. *"Snake's voice receded and my dream faded as I returned to ordinary life. But I felt his presence within me as a knowing which transcended the boundaries of time and space. It was a cup I would have had pass from me. The Pride preferred not to hear the premonitions of disaster I brought to the Circle of Elders. They turned a deaf ear to my prophecies and, I wonder now, why should they have listened? Was there anything any of us could have done?"*

The Panther's energy was heavy this particular night. And it filled the Lioness with a sense of foreboding, as though invisible hands were reaching into dark corners of her own life. *"The life I had always known, the life I had trusted would always be there, the life I had thought would be passed on to my cubs and their offspring after them, the intricate tapestry* that had been woven through generations of Panthers was about to unravel over the course of a few short seasons. I requested a special gathering of the Pride. We gathered on our sacred mountain. A gentle spring wind ruffled the fur on my back. I could hear the sound of crickets blending with the song of frogs. In the soft light of the moon I could see my friends, family, teachers, my whole life assembled in a circle around me.

'There are Strangers in our land,' I told the assembled group. 'There are Strangers in our land and the rumors we have heard from our relations in distant parts of the forest are coming home to touch our own sister, our own children, our own fathers. The fragrance of freedom inhaled by our parents and grandparents will now become the scent of fear breathed by our children and children's children. Murder is coming upon us, and slavery. We are entering dark times. But the dark times are not greater than the Light. We remember that without the light no shadow can be cast. A great shadow is about to fall upon our homeland. In this shadow we must remember what in the light we loved.'

I watched fear rise in the eyes of those ones I so dearly loved. My words were like a spear driving into my own heart! They did not recognize what slavery was. How can you know something of which you have no experience? No word? No concept? They shook their heads at me. They walked away. They did not understand.

And what they did not understand they feared. They came to fear me. I had been a respected member of my Pride, prepared from my earliest days to become a teacher and a leader. Now I was an outcast in the midst of them, an object of their scorn.

I sought the solace of solitude. I sought the spacious regions of the inner world, the inner life. Instead I found a desert. Everything I had come to believe I now came to doubt. All that I had come to value as true rose in my mind and in my heart to mock me as a lie. My own thoughts called me Fool, echoing the words spoken to me now by my own family. I remembered my dream and it appeared upon that inner desert like a shimmering mirage, a mere fantasy created by my overwhelming desire. I listened for the counsel of Snake and heard only the voice of my own doubt. The pride that had swelled in my chest, returning home from my quest, young and *full of the power of my dream, now withered in the wilderness like an over-ripe piece of fruit. It left a hard and wrinkled pit where a living heart once beat. In the center of that pit I knew, the one thing the Pride did not want to hear, the one thing I did not want to tell: that Death was coming upon us.*

In my dreams I saw the devastation that was to come. And in my waking I continued to cry out my warnings to the Pride. I tried to encourage them to prepare. But the more urgent my warnings, the deeper was the silence that returned to me, and the wider the distance between myself and all I loved.

Under the cover of night, one of the most respected elders, my beloved teacher came to me. He came as a friend and as a friend he encouraged me to keep silent. `Your words do not bring peace, but division,' he said. `They do not bring comfort but cut like a sword. There has not been such division among us, such fear and enmity, in my memory or in the memory of our Pride. You are too full of self-importance. You are full of the self-deceit from which pride blossoms. If truth were at work in your words, would not the truth in our own hearts rise up in recognition?'

I was hungry to hear his words, hungry to surrender the knowing of my own heart to his greater wisdom. His words were reasoned words, seasoned with many years of wise and gentle leadership. I had searched my own heart for an answer to this very question. Why indeed did the others not recognize the truth that had made itself known to me? And again a choice was before me.

'I cannot fail to speak the truth that has been given me. It is not for me to judge what is true for others but to be faithful to the knowing that lights my own path.' I said this hoping for understanding but knowing it was not what he had come into the night to obtain from me.

`What is Truth?' he said. It was not a question. It was a dismissal.

I watched him leave. I knew he would not return. It made no sense to me why I did not follow him, why I did not submit myself to his authority. But I did not. I remained in a darkness that invaded all of my senses. It perme-ated my thinking, my imagining and my feeling. I reached out with all my faculties to grasp the knowing within that held to the integrity of my choice. It eluded me.

Days passed and I fell deeper and deeper into a darkness of soul. I fell not into what was known but into what know me; not into anything I could grasp but into something that grasped me, that held me in benediction, that would never let me go.

'You are deluded,' were his parting words, the last words to be spoken to me by any member of the Pride until the days the Foreigners came upon us. By then it was too late."

The Black Panther paused in telling her story. She gazed intently into the eyes of the Lioness. *"It is a lonely journey, Silent One. The temptation is great to become someone other than ourselves, and many there are that take that path. The path is narrow that leads home. But it is not lonely for-ever…only for a little while. It can make all the difference to have a friend who can tell you that."*

The Silent One looked away from the eyes of her friend into the night sky. The stars were sharp and bright against the blackness. The sky was so like her friend, so like her eyes, so like her long supple body stretched out just beyond reach. Her eyes, her coat, her whole being reflected the starlight like a turning diamond refracts the Light. *"The Diamond One,"* she thought to herself, *"that's what she is to me."*

CHAPTER 25

It was several evenings later before The Diamond One resumed her story.

"*I was one of the survivors,*" she began. "*I got away with my life. But the months that followed were heavy with loss and with a sickening guilt that I was still breathing, still opening my eyes upon the dawn, when all whom I loved and cared for were dead or captured. I saw scenes over and over in my mind. In my waking and in my sleeping I saw the Foreigners close the trap they had cunningly laid for the members of my Pride.*

It was inevitable that the collective denial would eventually crack under the weight of evidence coming to us from cats who lived closer to that part of the coast where the Foreigners had first come ashore. They were fleeing up the shoreline and into the deeper forest, into our territory, with stories of horror. And with them the unsettled flight of birds and the warning calls of eagles alerted us to the presence of invaders in close pursuit. My clan pushed further and further into the jungle. But we did not realize that the canyon toward which we were heading for refuge was soon to become a death trap. The Foreigners had been there before us, digging pits lined with thick netting, setting guards at all possible escape routes. As the Pride approached the canyon we heard the wailing of many dogs rising up from behind us. Our adults formed a protective circle around the cubs and the old ones and hastened the pace toward the canyon. I was bringing up the rear of the circle when suddenly the forward line disappeared into the camouflaged pits. Suddenly all was confusion! Dogs came from every direction.

The Foreigners were exploding their Irons into the center of the circle where the elders were falling to the ground. Other Foreigners were capturing the ones with ropes and nets while still other cats were pursued and cornered by the hounding dogs!"

The Diamond One's voice was breaking. "I watched my own father, treed by dogs, was shot down by one of the Foreigners. I watched the dogs *tear his flesh and I was powerless to stop them, powerless to tear through the ropes that bound me!"*

The Panther's grief choked her voice. The Silent One never imagined that the Panther too carried such wounds. The Diamond One had seemed beyond such grief; beyond the raw sorrow that the Silent One now witnessed trembling through the Black Cat's entire body as her words stumbled into a low and mournful wail. The Lioness longed to reach out with her whole being to embrace her friend, to wrap her in the protective circle of her own body's warmth and make her safe.

But something else was stirring her. Alongside this tenderness rose an aggression, a desire to stop this telling, to stop the black anxiety now lapping at her own consciousness. But the Panther did not stop:

"I threw myself against the ropes with the entire strength of my body. With full focus of my will I fought but with each movement the ropes tightened, with each lunge the netting burned into my flesh."

The Silent One also felt the burning ropes across her own shoulders. Her own heart began to pound with a combination of fear and rage that gathered momentum in her muscles, that sparked like flashes of electricity through her nerves, that coursed like fire through her spine and burst in her mind's eye into image. The Silent One remembered! The images rushed in, tumbling one upon the other with a terrible clarity. She remembered her capture. She remembered her frantic running, running from the terrible image of her mother's death. And she remembered the moment before, the crispness of the air; the clean, cold exuberant breath that had filled her lungs; the pure vitality that had culminated into her Lioness roar. And then the answering retort. The explosion that shattered the air and shattered her life. The shot that had pursued her down through the years, haunting her dreams, igniting panic in her veins, imposing submission, demanding that she pay for that roar which brought the wrath of death upon her beloved mother.

And how she had paid! Submissive and silent beneath the hand of the Keepers, she atoned for a crime that was not hers. "The Silent One," they had called her and counted on her silence to cover the multiplication of their crimes. She saw it all as though looking into a sphere of crystal. She saw her young innocence at the sphere's center. She saw the ensuing events of her life reverberating like waves flowing into the present circle of her existence. And it all flowed from a cub's misconception. She was not responsible for her mother's murder! It was not her roar that mysteriously drew the deathblow to her mother's living body. And her silence now could never bring her mother back.

Way down in her deepest core it began. It coursed through her backbone. It spread hot into her pelvis. It retched in her belly at the memory of her mother's death. And yet it continued, slicing up though her heart (cutting away the proud flesh), up through her throat, (the sound of dogs yapping at her ears). And still it rose, like a serpentine fire, cleaving her skull at the place between her eyes, splitting the darkness with its searing sound, rising out of her flesh, out of the silence of her life, to wake her sleeping dead. Finally her roar exploded into the world!

CHAPTER 26

The roar of the Lioness woke the Keepers from their sleep. It woke cats all across the compound. Down the steep cliff walls into the valley of the male cats it reached, and beyond. The Coyotes ceased their howling to listen. And the wind carried it even to the dwellings of Strangers that littered the desert floor many miles distance from the Preserve. It gave a haunting rattle to their windows and a shiver to their hearts. It was a voice unlike any that had been heard before. It hovered over the great expanse of land and hearts and held eternity in its breath. Then it receded back into silence.

In this pregnant silence the two cats rested. Their whole being now open one to the other, they touched. No more words were spoken. The Lioness knew what happened to the Panther after her capture. It was her own story: imprisonment, abuse, and degradation. But the difference was The Diamond One had remembered her Self. And that had made all the difference. Now the Lioness also remembered. She realized that this Self-remembering did not exempt her from suffering. In the world of beginnings and endings there would always be suffering. But now her suffering had meaning. A communion of soul had grown between the two friends. It thrust through the common soil of their suffering into a shared remembrance and found roots in realms beyond time.

CHAPTER 27

❀

Suns rose and suns set. Cold hard nights turned tender. The bare desert landscape blossomed into color. Cricket song filled the air. Snakes, roused from their wintry sleep, stretched in the sun on flat rocks. Against the backdrop of such a day, when the wind was soft and warm upon her back, The Diamond One approached the Lioness, and said:

"This is a season of new beginnings. According to the teachings of the Ancient Ones it is a good season for entering the Dream. You have yet to seek your vision, my friend." The Lioness remembered the story of the Panther's own vision, her departure from the Pride, her lonely wandering, her meeting with Snake.

"But I cannot make a journey into the wilderness. How can I seek a vision when I am caged?" The Diamond One could hear the yearning in the Lioness' voice. The ancient rite had roots far back in the history of the Lioness' own race. Now that primal memory rose up in the Lioness, gleaming in her eyes as she looked hopefully into her friend's face.

"You are already in the wilderness," The Diamond One responded. *"Besides, visions come from within...and beyond. I will help you."* She directed her to fast for three days and three nights. *"During that time drink only water. Keep silence in your heart. Turn your gaze inward. Allow your inner ear to open."* She said she would not visit her until the end of the three days. Then she would come and together they would intone the ancient chant and draw the sacred circle. *"I will be holding you in my heart, my friend,"* she said, and departed.

The Lioness did as she was counseled. It was so very difficult, this turning inward. Now that the floodgates of memory had opened, image upon image unfolded in her mind's eye. She could not shake them. The terrifying images awakened fear in her. She hated this fear. She hated herself for having this fear. And she could not tolerate it. She would float away from it into fantasies of power and revenge. She saw herself doing to the Keepers what they had done to her. She spent her fear in hatred towards them, spinning scene upon scene of murder and domination and abuse upon those who had murdered her mother, who had dominated and abused her. And through it all she felt justified. She saw herself as some kind of hero, exacting justice on her own behalf and on behalf of those who could not or would not fight for themselves. But the relief she found in these fantasies was fleeting. Returning hatred for hatred could never bring true justice. This yearning for truth, this yearning for justice kept calling her deeper, calling her to face her fear and to move through it.

As she practiced tolerating the fear, tender memories began to surface. She remembered herself as a small cub. She remembered the absolute trust she had in life, the openness of her heart towards all of life. She remembered the warmth of her mother's belly, the comfort. All had been right with the world. And then it all became so wrong! She was wrong! She lived it again: her roar, the shot, her terror, the closing down of her heart! Never to be tender again! Never to be vulnerable again! Never to be innocent again! She saw how her heart closed. And she wept for that tender heart, for that tender cub, for that great loss of her life. She wept until she was spent. And then she slept.

All the next day she drifted in and out of sleep. She felt despair. Despair at the loss of her innocence, at the loss of her heart, at the anger that ran through her being as fundamental as the blood that flowed in her veins. She saw her anger, its meanness and its callousness. She saw all the ways she had fooled herself into believing that she was powerful when in fact she was a wall of defenses against the actual fact of her powerlessness. She floated between this despair and the sleep of self-forgetting into the third day.

Remembering her friend's counsel, she fought the sleep that made her body feel drugged and heavy. She roused herself and gathered all of her energy and again turned inward. Again the currents of thought, fantasy and emotion rose in that inner space. She let them rise. But gradually she began to notice that they also fell away. They fell away and back toward the Source from which they came. She followed them back. The long familiar lava-flow of her passions branched into arteries of fear and reservoirs of hurt and still there was something more…something other. She followed the energy of her life, energy she had wasted for so many years with bitter anger. She followed it back and down. It became the gateway to her soul. There her rage touched a wider innocence. There her anger touched a greater truth. There her passion learned compassion. There she rested until the Diamond One came.

CHAPTER 28

ॶॶ

The Diamond One intoned the chant that had come through the generations from the Ancient Ones. As she began the chant, all the Cats who had chanted it before, each of whom had taken their own solitary journey in quest of their own Dream, were called in spirit to become a part of the sacred circle. A cloud of witnesses became present, a multitude of invisible allies were called forth, as the Lioness joined her voice with the Panther's. The chant spiraled from tones deep in the belly into notes of trembling tenderness and trebling pathos. It crescendoed and fell to its own quiet completion. The Lioness was then instructed to pad out a circle, walking three times around its circumference. That done, she settled within its center.

As she had done for the Lioness so many times before, the Panther now did again. She told her a story. Deep and slow, rising and falling in rhythm with the Lioness' breath, the Panther's voice helped the golden cat beyond her cage:

"*It's been a long time that you have wandered, lost in the wilderness. But now a great mountain rises in the distance. Its peak is lost in the clouds.*" The voice of the Panther spiraled like the chant, drawing the Lioness into the story and up towards the mountain. "*As you come to its base you find a narrow trail worn into the rock by the hooves of deer…You sense the trail beneath your footpads…and you follow…up and up…until the trail branches out into many separate paths. There is no one to tell you which path to take. You must decide for yourself. And you do decide…you make a choice…and you continue. There are times you experience great hunger…times of great thirst…but you persist…winding your way up and up into the clouds. Eventually the cloud becomes so thick that you feel you are surely lost. Still you go on…blindly…not knowing why…knowing only the desire that propels you onward, drawn by the vision that must lie ahead. Finally you reach the top. And now, in this place of power, you again draw your circle."*

Through the threshold of the story the Lioness had indeed journeyed up the mountain. She padded out her circle, three times, as she had been instructed and sat within its center. It was a circle within a great circle. She looked into the circle of sky above her and into the circle of space that surrounded her. It was truly spectacular! Behind her and far below lay soft, jade hills. She could see rivers, like turquoise threads winding between the slopes and pooling in jeweled lakes that reflected the sun. Green and undulating hills rolled down toward the desert that was blanketed by a thick white cover of cloud. She could not see the Preserve, the Prisons, the pettiness and meanness from here, only the softness extending toward the horizon. On either side of her the spine of the mountain range thrust itself up toward the sky, baring its raw boned courage to the elements while wind-blown trees clung tenaciously to fissured rock many feet below. Before her the mountain dropped precipitously down into a granite basin of lakes and waterfalls. Fir and Pine forests grew up between the lakes, circled lush meadows, then marched up canyons towards yet higher mountains eternally snow-capped and silent.

So much beauty! So much magnificence! And yet her heart did not swell to meet it. Her heart was like a dead thing inside of her. She felt a great emptiness overtake her. Never had she felt more alone. It was into this loneliness she dropped, deeper and deeper, until she entered her Dream.

She was seeking shelter from the cold in a cave upon a windy crag of mountain. The cave was littered with rock, musky with dampness and strewn with broken webs. She pawed at the rock, circling and scratching at the earth to clear a space where she might sleep. It was then that she discovered the chest. It was very old. Metal straps carved with an indecipherable language laced its edges and a heavy padlock, broken by falling rocks, had sealed its contents. It was a chest full of secrets, abandoned here many years before. The years had left its accumulation of dust upon its surface. Stones had nearly buried it beneath their weight. Here, as in a grave, it waited.

She pawed and nudged the stones away until she could reach the padlock. As she cleared the dust from the lid and marveled at the unknown language she heard their words being spoken in her mind: *"This is the place where you put the things that you forgot."* She opened the chest and in it was a dead cub, dead but still alive, all eyes, and the eyes were looking at her.

At first she felt numb, as dead and unfeeling as the small lion-cub. But again the words spoke: *"This is the place where you put the things that you forgot."* Now her heart accelerated, faster and faster it began to beat as her breath became short and she began to weep. She wept without reason, without thought, and her weeping carried her back down the mountain, through the desert, back to the valley of her beginnings. And still she wept.

The words came again, a third time: *"This is the place where you put the things that you forgot."* And looking into the cub's eyes she felt herself pulled into the chest, into the pain of her mother's death, into the terror of being held in the net, into the despair of powerlessness, until the chest broke open. She beheld herself standing within it, a powerful Lioness, surrounded with a soft glowing light. She looked at that poor cub, buried and alone for so long, and saw in that cub her own most vulnerable and tender self. With absolute love she cradled her to her breast.

And the cub spoke:

"I am the hidden core, the hidden meaning. When you see me clearly, then you will know your Self. You will know compassion because I am the clear center that reflects the Truth. I am the mirror. I am the innocence against which all your deceit is revealed. I am the child whose innocence you could not tolerate, whose purity you could not sustain. This is the way of evil in the world. But before evil was, I AM."

The cub then touched the heart of the Lioness who felt herself dissolve through the rock of the cave, a nearly intolerable lightness suffusing her being. She felt herself dissolve into Space, into a deep velvet peace that held her and called her by name. And the events that had shaped her life, the painful memories she had locked in her heart, were a tiny speck of glittering in that vast space. Finally she knew: She was so much bigger than that frightened cub; so much greater than that time bound Lioness. Evil did not define her. She was free.

CHAPTER 29

The Lioness returned from her journey. She awakened in her cage. But it no longer held her. She had grown bigger than her prison. Her friend, The Diamond One, was waiting in her usual place beside the cell. For a long time neither spoke. Finally the Lioness said:

"I have found my path, Diamond One. It is the path of compassion." She paused a moment, then added. "My vision showed me that a cub will lead me upon it." A warm and comfortable silence rose up to surround the two great Cats as each saw in the eyes of the other two fiery suns spinning around black centers of infinite peace.

"My vision revealed something else." The Lioness settled firmly upon her powerful haunches. She took a deep breath and as her great chest expanded a slight breeze caressed the downy white and yellow hairs upon her breast. "I have found my teacher," she said to her friend. "It is my own heart."

Together they gazed out over the compound. The Lioness held all present within her gaze: the Cats and the Keepers, and beyond, the Strangers in whose world her cubs were embarked upon their own life's journey. She held the lion, pacing in captivity just a short distance away. She held all the pain and all the sorrow of her life and the lives of those she had touched. None was bigger than her own heart.

Out of the expansiveness of her heart the roar gathered. It sprang from a place of innocent truth inside her. "I AM" she roared her name into the world. "I AM" she roared the name from which she came. "I

AM" she roared the name to which she would return. "Before Evil was, I AM." ~